The King

Who ate my Breakfast!

Edward Glover

Published in the United Kingdom by:

Blue Falcon Publishing
The Mill, Pury Hill Business Park,
Alderton Road, Towcester
Northamptonshire
NN12 7LS
Email: books@bluefalconpublishing.co.uk
Web: www.bluefalconpublishing.co.uk

A CIP record of this book is available from the British Library.

First printed November 2021

ISBN 978-1912765478

For Louis

Edward Glover

Chapter
1

Louis was an energetic, ambitious and very kind boy, though sometimes impatient if things didn't quite go his way. But then, aren't we all impatient from time to time?

However, the most singular thing about Louis was that, no matter how tired he may have been after a busy day, he always woke the next morning at the same time – seven o'clock. He was as punctual as a railway timetable. That was commendable on a school day. But he even got up early on a Saturday and, more surprising still, on a Sunday, including in wintertime, when

sensible people prefer to stay warm in bed for that little bit longer.

Louis simply couldn't help it.

Once, his mother hid his bedside clock so he couldn't see the time. But he found where she had hidden it. On another occasion, she put his clock back thirty minutes. As usual, though, he checked the kitchen clock before he went to bed, so rumbled what she had done, and after she said goodnight he changed the bedside clock to the correct time. She even pretended that the battery in his clock was dead. It made no difference. Somehow he still knew it was time to get up. He would throw back the bedclothes, put on his dressing gown and slippers, and go downstairs for his breakfast, which was always prepared the night before. Such was the organised house in which he lived.

One day, after supper, Louis sat in his bedroom to do his homework. The day hadn't gone right. He'd got wet going to school and on the way home. Even worse than that, when he'd opened his school bag to give his empty lunch box to his mother, his brightly coloured pencil case was missing. He must have left it in his classroom tray or perhaps it had dropped out of his

school bag as he walked – and ran and skipped and puddle-jumped – home. His mother had told him off for not closing it properly.

"You're always losing things, Louis. Buck up. Pay attention to what you're doing. You've got to be more careful."

Her words ringing in his ears, he switched on the table lamp. He disliked this time of the year intensely, even though it included his birthday – he'd just turned ten.

Summer had disappeared long ago, gloomy autumn had arrived, and ghastly winter lurked around the corner. The thought of homework demanding his attention lowered his spirits even further. But there was a ray of brightness. The half-term break – ten whole days – was not far away. He, his older sister, Agnes, and his younger brother, Raffy, were going to stay with their grandparents in their big old house in the country. They had been to the house before. Louis enjoyed being there for all sorts of reasons, not least the large garden, with its swing – a comfortable cocoon hanging from a great walnut tree in which he could read a book, if he felt so inclined – and a trampoline.

It also had a tennis court. Most of all he liked having breakfast early with his grandfather in the oak-beamed dining room, sitting at a refectory table that dated back to the beginning of the English Civil War. (Louis was keen on history and knew that this had started in 1642.) Everything would be neatly laid out, waiting for his arrival. And, of course, the table candles would be lit. Louis's breakfasts at home were good, but those his grandfather prepared were extra scrumptious – more

fruit and either a croissant or pain au chocolat to follow. What a delight! A small helping would be set for Raffy, too, for the once-in-a-blue-moon occasions when he joined his brother in venturing downstairs early. The thought of that mouth-watering abundance of blueberries, raspberries and strawberries, topped with creamy yogurt, cheered Louis greatly, but he still had to get through the next week. Why did time take so long to pass?

He stood up and looked out of the window. It was a dismal scene. Darkness was already falling, big raindrops slid down the panes of glass and the tree in the garden was almost leafless. He sighed, sat down once more at the small table close to his bed, slowly opened his bag, pulled out a red exercise book – damp and battered – and began his maths homework. He didn't mind maths. Mrs Armitage, his teacher, said he was good at it. He quickly completed all twelve

questions, checked his answers and, satisfied he'd got most of them right, closed the book. He put it on the radiator to dry.

After answering some geography questions – all easy-peasy – he took his violin from its case, practised some scales, then played a short tune he would be performing solo at the school concert towards the end of term. He heard his mother call out that it would soon be bath time. Louis knew he could no longer put off finding out what half-term homework his English teacher, Mr Webb, had set. Reluctantly, he opened the exercise book. He knew what the task would be – it was one he disliked the most. He came to the page. There it was in bright-red ink:

During half-term, please write a story. It can be

about anything – something you did, or where you went, or inspired by what you read. Use your imagination. And it has to include at least 10 words you've not used before.

Louis's heart sank. He enjoyed all his school subjects but writing a story was so boring. Yes, he could make up a story if he was told what to write about. But to invent a story without any suggestion – well, that was asking too much. He looked at the books on the shelf above the table. They were all well-known. He couldn't copy any of their ideas. He had to find one of his own. His mother often said he should use his imagination. He wasn't sure what it looked like or where he could find it. He enjoyed reading books but to think up a story of his own – that feat eluded him. His mind just didn't click.

That night he lay in bed thinking about his English homework. Perhaps he could write about his bedside clock. He looked at the luminous dial. His grandfather had told him once that the hardest part about writing a story was composing the first sentence. It was like finding the source of a river. Once you'd done that, he said, you could get into a boat and let the river carry you along. Louis stared at the clock, urging it to give him inspiration. It didn't. The big hand just moved forward, silently and relentlessly, minute after minute.

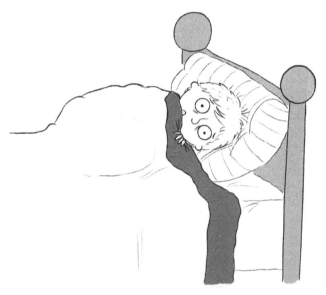

The following day, the day after that and for the rest of the week, on the way to school and on the way home, Louis thought hard about the story he had to write. The more he thought, the crosser he got. His mother persistently asking him if he had decided what to write about only increased his frustration. If only he could find his imagination. Half-term arrived and he still hadn't found it. Mr Webb's parting words to the class echoed in his head: "Happy half-term everyone. I'm looking forward to reading your stories."

Louis loved playing cricket. He was good at it. But delivering an idea for a story had so far stumped him – no runs on the scoreboard.

Chapter

2

Louis followed the same routine every evening when he came to stay in his grandparents' old house: supper, a bath, a bedtime story from his grandfather, followed by a poem from him, and, most important of all, a last check of the bedside clock. To be on time for the daily treat of a delicious breakfast, he made absolutely sure the night before, when his grandfather came to read to him, that the bedside clock showed the correct time.

On the first evening of his half-term visit, since he had left his own watch downstairs to charge, Louis peeked at his grandfather's watch. This way he could still be sure that the bedside clock was accurate and thus he would not be late for breakfast.

Just as his grandfather was leaving the bedroom, Louis decided to pop the question.

"I've got to write a story for school. I have some ideas of my own but I wondered, if you had any, whether we could talk about them over breakfast in the morning."

"Maybe, Louis. Let's see what the morning brings. Of

course, I would be interested to hear your ideas first."

Louis winced. Fibs easily catch you out.

His mother came in to say goodnight and put the light out.

"Tomorrow, Louis, you really must begin your English homework. You have to write that story. There's no escaping it."

Louis nodded. The task that confronted him was like a tiresome fly buzzing around his head in the summer.

The next morning – it was a Monday – Louis woke up early as always. He noticed it was a little darker than usual but, looking at the illuminated dial, he saw it was almost seven o'clock. He got out of bed, put on his dressing gown and slippers, and, ensuring he did not wake his older sister in the bed next to his, tiptoed to the door and along the upstairs corridor, past the other bedrooms. At the top of the staircase he stopped and listened. There wasn't a sound, other than his tummy rumbling loudly, so hungry was he – constant hunger was another of Louis's defining traits. He went quietly downstairs, careful not to tread on the middle step, which always creaked. Standing in the front hall, he could hear voices coming from the dining room. Probably his grandfather, listening to the early-morning news on the radio as he often did. Louis slowly pushed back the half-open door.

To his astonishment, instead of his grandfather, someone else was sitting at the head of the table – an old man with twinkling eyes and crinkly grey hair down to his shoulders. He wore a rich-blue velvet jacket, edged in gold brocade, beneath which was a

breastplate, glinting in the candlelight.

Most extraordinary of all, on his head a golden crown perched askew. Louis stood in the doorway, rooted to the spot, speechless. It was the first time he had ever seen a king in person – assuming of course the figure at the table was a king. But who else would wear a crown except a king? Then again, as kings normally lived in palaces, what was this king doing here?

And he was not alone. At the other end of the table, in the candles' lambent glow, sat an elegant lady in a long yellow gown with puff sleeves, a blue shawl tightly drawn around her shoulders.

They looked up, suddenly aware of Louis's presence on the threshold.

"Who are you?" said the king irritably. He didn't like being interrupted when eating his breakfast.

"I'm Louis."

"Hmm," muttered the king. "Listen, young man, first things first. You should call me Your Majesty. After all, I'm a king. And, by the way, you should bow. That's another thing you should do when you meet a king for the first time."

"Yes, Your Majesty," replied Louis, bowing deeply.

"But you don't have to touch your toes when you bow," said the king.

"Yes, Your Majesty," repeated Louis, nodding his head while at the same time wondering whether he should have said, "No, Your Majesty," and now absolutely terrified.

"Have you anything else to say for yourself?" said the king, spectacles poised precariously on the tip of his long slender nose. He beckoned Louis to come closer. "Have you a question? It looks as though you have one in your mouth but it's not coming out. Come on, ask me. I don't bite."

"Please, Your Majesty, what is your name?"

"I thought you would have known. I am King Ludwig of Hesse-Darmstadt – the ninth of that name. Ring any bells, my boy?"

"No. I don't ring any bells," answered Louis nervously. "There aren't any in the house."

The king tutted. "I meant bells in your head."

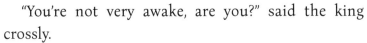

"I don't have any in my head," replied Louis.

"You're not very awake, are you?" said the king crossly.

"It's too early to be really awake," admitted Louis.

The king harrumphed.

"Sir, you just asked me about bells. I forgot about this one." Louis walked to the side of the fireplace and pressed a button in the wall. There was a distant tinkling sound from the kitchen. "Once upon a time there were servants in the house, but now they're all gone."

"I've already noticed," growled the king. "When I called for some service, no one came to take away my plate. What are things coming to?"

"That's the way things are for those like me who don't live in palaces," said

Louis.

"Enough of bells and palaces. What's your name again, boy?"

"My name is Louis."

"I see. You've got the same name as that pompous French popinjay, the one who claimed he was the Sun King. An objectionable man, who couldn't keep his hands off other people's lands. Just like that other pushy king, Frederick the so-called Great of Prussia. He was an even worse thief. Look, that's him on the wall. But he's far too proud to mix with the likes of us."

Louis looked perplexed – and embarrassed, as his tummy was rumbling even more loudly.

"Where was I? Oh yes, I was talking about Louis Quatorze – you know, Louis the Fourteenth. He was around a long time. Nobody really liked him. Any relation?"

"I don't think so."

"But aren't you a Louis too? Except in German it's Ludwig – a much better version, surely?"

"If you say so, sir."

"I do. Now that we've established we share the same name, though spelled differently – and mind you, that's important – perhaps we can talk about something else.

By the way, I'm going to call you Ludwig."

"Of course, Your Majesty."

"Ludwig, do you own any land?"

"No, sir. But my parents own the house we live in."

"And where's that house?"

"In London."

"And who owns this house?"

"My grandparents."

"Not a bad place but a bit draughty and certainly not as big as my palace," mused the king.

"Where's your palace?" asked Louis, gaining in confidence.

"In Germany, several days from here – perhaps a week or more – by horse-drawn coach. I haven't seen any go past yet."

"They won't because no coaches like that come here," explained Louis. "Only buses stop in the village."

"I don't know what a bus is," said the king grumpily.

"It's got an engine –"

"Ludwig, I think you should answer Louis's question," interrupted the lady in the shawl.

"What was Ludwig's question?"

"He wanted to know where you live. Not just how far away it is."

The king shuffled in his chair – or rather, in Louis's

17

grandfather's chair.

"I used to live in a splendid palace in the centre of Germany, from which I governed my own lands. I had lots of servants and an army too. But now I live there."

He pointed to high up on the wall.

All Louis could see in the gloom was a large empty picture frame.

"I usually come down to stretch my legs after everyone has gone to bed. But this morning, young Ludwig, you appeared too early, before I'd had a chance to return. According to my pocket watch, which is now very old, like me, it's only six o'clock, not seven. So, that's why I'm here and not up there. And the same goes for Lady St George, who steps out of her frame to keep me company."

Louis found it even harder to believe what he was seeing and hearing.

"Young man, you're doing it again Your mouth is wide open but no words are coming out. If you don't say something soon, I suggest you close it. Otherwise you might swallow a fly."

"Ludwig, don't be so beastly to him."

"I'm sorry," said the king, not sounding contrite at all. "I'm in one of my moods."

"As we can all see!" said Lady St George.

Louis finally summoned the courage to speak.

"Your Majesty, I think you've eaten my breakfast. And the lady has eaten my brother's."

"Oh dear! Was that your breakfast?" exclaimed the king. "I was so hungry. After all, I haven't eaten since I popped my clogs two hundred and twenty-nine years ago, and after such an eternity the craving becomes a crisis of epic proportion. It was delicious. I especially liked the small berries and the cream."

"It's not cream, Your Majesty," replied Louis, able neither to stop the constant rumbling in his stomach nor to suppress any longer his irritation about losing his breakfast – he could scarcely survive not eating for 229 minutes, let alone 229 years.

"What is it, then?"

"It's yogurt and it comes from goat's milk. And the berries are blueberries."

"I've not had yuggy before. It was rather tasty."

Lady St George smiled at Louis. "We apologise for eating what was not ours to eat. But we were famished. As His Majesty said, we haven't eaten for years. Every evening we look down at what all of you are tucking into. It always looks mouth-wateringly tempting."

Louis sighed. "It doesn't matter. I'm glad you enjoyed it," he said, resigned to going without his breakfast and trying not to think about how long he would have to wait until lunchtime.

"We really did," said Lady St George, putting a comforting arm around Louis. "And though you may not think so, it has helped put His Majesty in a better mood this morning. Sometimes he's grumpy – occasionally very grumpy. But this morning he found something to eat after many years of nothing. And, I might add, he's been rather greedy, because he took some of what I found, which was already a smaller portion than his. So, while he's satisfied, I'm still a little hungry."

"Would you like some more?" asked Louis, remembering his mother's instructions always to be very polite to ladies, and wondering how he was going to tell his brother that his breakfast had gone.

"What a kind boy you are, Louis. Yes, please."

Louis turned towards the kitchen.

"He's not Louis, he's Ludwig," the king bellowed.

"Ludwig, keep your voice down," shushed Lady St George.

"But I didn't say anything," said Louis.

"No, Louis, I wasn't speaking to you. I was telling His Majestic Grumpiness to lower his."

"I'll be back in a moment," said Louis.

He went into the kitchen and found his grandfather's breakfast in the larder, ready to eat. He was sure his grandfather wouldn't mind if he borrowed some of it for the hungry lady. He took a bowl and a plate from the cupboard, choosing yellow to match the colour of her dress. Then he filled the bowl with some berries and yogurt and put on the plate the remaining croissant, which he knew had been saved for his mother. He placed the plate and bowl on a tray, carried it into the dining room and, with a bow, offered its contents to Lady St George.

"Thank you," she said.

"I'm pleased to be of service," replied Louis.

"You remind me of my son when he was young. But

21

he didn't dress like you. Why don't you fetch some breakfast for yourself and come and sit with us? You can tell us about your brother and sister."

Louis hesitated. Lady St George insisted.

"Please do join us. Before long it will be light and then we'll have to return to our frames on the wall."

"I agree," said the king, adding in between burps that he thought he had eaten too much.

So, after finding some other things to eat, Louis sat down at the dining table – the king on his right and Lady St George on his left. He was very nervous. After all, he had never eaten breakfast with a king before. He

told them about Raffy and Agnes. Then King Ludwig and Lady St George asked him lots of questions about school, and he told them all about cricket, taekwondo, swimming, running and football. They listened attentively, the king's eyes getting bigger and bigger in astonishment. He found it particularly hard to understand the rules of cricket.

And so they talked, about countless things. As they did, it began to get lighter and lighter outside.

Chapter
3

Louis woke. Daylight was peeping around the edge of the window blind. The bedside clock said seven. Still sleepy from the late night before, he got up, a little unsure where he was. A moment ago, surely, he had been sitting in the dining room eating breakfast with a king and a beautiful lady in a yellow gown. He looked at his sister, still asleep. After putting on his dressing gown and slippers, he crept from the room, along the corridor and then downstairs to the dining room. He pushed open the door in great trepidation. His grandfather
emerged from the kitchen with a mug of tea. Louis looked at the table. There was his breakfast, neatly laid out  ready for him. And it was uneaten!

"Good morning, Louis," said his grandfather. "I hope you slept well. Would you like to have a croissant after your fruit and yogurt? That will leave two – one for your brother and another for your mummy. Oh! I forgot to bring you your glass of water. I'll go and get it."

His grandfather disappeared into the kitchen. Louis turned to the portrait of King Ludwig high up on the wall behind him and looked at it intently. He was sure the king winked at him. Then he looked at Lady St George, above the doorway to the television room. Surely she smiled at him. He turned again to study the

king – stern and grumpy. But something was not quite right. There on his breastplate was a pearl of yogurt-coated blueberry. Louis pointed to it.

The king looked down, mouthed the words "thank you", flicked the yogurt and the berry onto his finger and licked them off. Louis turned back to Lady St George. Smiling and shrugging her shoulders, she put a finger to her lips. Louis knew that meant he had to keep a very important secret to himself – about the morning he had eaten breakfast with King Ludwig of Hesse-Darmstadt and Lady St George. Or was it just a dream? He couldn't be sure.

His grandfather returned with a glass of water and sat down at the table.

"We're suddenly rather low on yogurt, berries and croissants. I'm sure there were more last night. But it's not a problem. I've added them to this morning's shopping list."

Louis said nothing. He just smiled.

The next morning, while his grandfather was making fresh tea in the kitchen, Louis looked up at King Ludwig's portrait. There was no sign of the smudge of yogurt from the day before. The king just sat motionless and dour in the picture frame as he had done for the past two hundred and fifty years, since the artist applied the last stroke of paint. Louis shrugged. What he thought had happened yesterday – the royal theft of his breakfast – must surely have been a dream.

"Oh well," he murmured. "Dreams can play funny tricks."

He decided to say nothing about it. He didn't want anyone to think he was losing his marbles at such a young age. Besides, as his mother often said about past events that went wrong, it's water under the bridge. Move on, she would add, though he sometimes wondered what that really meant in his case. Move on to where?

That evening he went to bed at the usual time of eight o'clock. His grandfather read him a story and Louis read his grandfather a poem in return. His

mother tucked him up, and his sister Agnes too, who was in the next bed, then put out the bedside light, warning Louis yet again not to go downstairs for his breakfast before seven o'clock. In the darkness of the room, he reflected on another day that had been and gone. He considered it to have been energetic – sailing in the morning, an after-lunch walk, a visit to the play park and in the late afternoon some practice in the cricket nets. Yes, it had been a busy day. The mere recollection of what he had done led him to feel tired and soon he began to drift off to sleep, but not before thinking of the pain au chocolat he had been promised for breakfast the next morning.

❦ ❦ ❦ ❦ ❦

Louis became aware of a hissing buzz in his ear. "Psst! Psst! Psst!" He struggled to open his eyes. In the dim light cast by the lamp on the landing he saw a figure bending over him. He suddenly realised it was the king.

"Ludwig, wake up. We've got a long way to go," whispered the ancient monarch. "Here are some clothes. Put them on and meet me downstairs. Quickly now, my carriage is waiting for us." The king disappeared in a puff of dust from being immobile for so long.

Louis looked at his bedside clock. It was four in the morning – three hours before he was due to get up. But accepting that kings had to be obeyed, he gathered his wits and got out of bed, just as the king reappeared.

"Hurry up, Ludwig. If we don't leave in the next five minutes, we'll be late for lunch."

"But, Your Majesty, it's only four o'clock. I'm not supposed to go downstairs before seven. And what about my breakfast? Breakfast comes before lunch."

"We're not having breakfast downstairs, Ludwig, we are going to eat at my place, the palace. Please hurry up and get dressed. I can smell the food already and I'm ravenously hungry." And he disappeared again.

Louis scooped up the clothes the king had dropped at the end of his bed and went into the bathroom to avoid waking his sister, though it was a miracle she hadn't woken already given the noise the royal visitor had made. In place of his pyjamas he put on a white high-collared shirt, yellow stockings held up with garters, knee-length blue breeches and a red waistcoat with silver buttons. Over that he put on a blue frock coat with gold trim. Finally, he slipped on shiny black shoes, each with a large bright silver buckle. He was thankful he didn't normally have to wear such fussy and complicated clothes. The wig was an encumbrance too far,

though, and he stuffed it in his coat pocket.

He crept along the corridor and downstairs. The king and Lady St George were waiting for him by the front door. Ludwig nodded his approval of Louis's sartorial transformation, then frowned when he noticed his bare head. "Wig," he said, peremptorily. Louis was about to argue but, seeing the king's expression, thought better of it. Duly peruked, he turned to more practical matters.

"Your Majesty, that door is rarely unlocked. If we're leaving the house, we'll have to use the kitchen door. I know where the spare key is kept – in a pot on the windowsill."

"Leave by the back door! Kings don't do that. We make grand entrances and exits by the front door."

"Ludwig, don't be so pompous," Lady St George reproved.

"Are you talking to me or him?" snapped the king.

"To you. You're the one making the fuss – and unnecessary fuss at that. Besides, if you carry on being stamp-foot sulky you'll waste time and wake everyone else. As you are hungry, let's get going by using the kitchen door."

Louis retrieved the key and all three left the house by the kitchen door, the king muttering under his breath that never in his life had he suffered the indignity of leaving a building by the back door. Louis led the way to the front of the house, where, on the

forecourt, stood a magnificent golden carriage with six white horses, each bearing a tall plume of red feathers. Pawing at the gravel, they were clearly anxious to set off.

The king got in first, knocking his crown awry, followed by Lady St George. As Louis was about to climb in, the king exclaimed, "But we've forgotten the most important thing!"

Louis looked puzzled.

"Ludwig, Louis, whatever your name is – oh dear! I

get so confused with names these days – we haven't got your bats!"

"Sir," Louis replied, "I don't keep bats. There are some that live in the church down the road, though. Would you like to go and see them?"

"Silly boy, I mean that piece of wood you hit a ball with, in the baffling game you were telling us about. I've seen you playing with it in the dining room – not that you're supposed to. Go and get it, boy, and the ball too. Don't stand gawping, Ludwig. Go and get them. Hurry!"

Once Louis was finally in the carriage with the cricket bat across his knees and the ball in his coat pocket, the disgruntled king gave the order and the coach lurched forward onto the road.

Fortunately, at that early hour there was no car or van to crash into, or driver to be bewildered by this extraordinary sight.

Louis didn't take in many details of the journey. Half the time they seemed to be flying across a dark sky and the other half he was sleeping, dreaming of the long-awaited pain au chocolat. He was used to getting up early, but not at four o'clock in the morning! And the king's grumpiness made matters worse. He was still grumbling about the shame of leaving by the back door a house that had been his home for the past fifteen years. After a while, echoing the words in Louis's head, Lady St George told the king to stop complaining and to either go to sleep or talk about something else.

Chapter
4

Eventually, they arrived. Louis had expected a castle but instead he saw a stately palace, resplendent in the sunshine. Bewigged servants rushed to welcome the king and his guests. As they entered the palace through the grand front entrance, Louis looked back to see a long green lawn spread either side of a central gravel avenue lined with trees. This would be an excellent spot to create a wicket and teach the king to bat.

"Come on, Ludwig, don't dawdle. We've got to eat before you show me how to play your peculiar game."

"Yes, Your Majesty," Louis replied, his breakfast-deprived tummy rumbling more loudly than ever.

A flotilla of footmen escorted them to somewhere called the Long Dining Room – and certainly it seemed many times as long as the one in which his grandfather served breakfast. The king sat at one end of the vast

table, Lady St George at the other. Louis sat midway between the two. The king bellowed to be heard, making Lady St George wince, while she herself spoke softly. This resulted in the king asking one of the footmen to run with his words to the other end of the table and return with her reply. Louis had never seen such a ridiculous situation before.

By this time, Louis's hunger was intense. Memories of his supper the night before were no longer sufficient to ward off the pangs he was experiencing. He heard his tummy say, "Louis, I'm getting cross. Where is my breakfast?"

Suddenly, there was a strident clang. Louis turned and looked up at a great clock on the wall. It was striking midday! With a blaring fanfare, the doors at the end of the dining room opened. A braid-swagged official of the court entered, thundering, "Lunch is served, Majesty!" followed by a long line of footmen balancing large trays of food. "What happened to breakfast?" asked Louis's tummy, crosser than ever. The footmen laid tray after tray on the table, each one piled

high with meat, fish, poultry, bread, cheese, marmalade and sauerkraut. But there was no yogurt, no raspberries, no blueberries and no strawberries. Then to add to the bedlam, a small orchestra began to play in the gallery above. Music, a bellowing king, a thundering grandee, the clangs of the clock still striking midday and the clatter of silver trays were

almost too much for Louis to bear. His unhappiness was all the greater because the pain au chocolat he had been patiently waiting for was nowhere to be seen.

"Ludwig, eat well and quickly because within the hour you're going to teach me how to play cricket."

Louis nodded and, though crestfallen that his favourite breakfast was missing, he took some meat and cheese. The meat was thick and salty and the cheese hard. He chewed as best he could, trying to give a convincing impression that he was eating a lot. Lady St George sent a whisper down the table: "Do your best, Louis."

Having devoured the huge mound of food with

which he had laden his silver plate, the king proclaimed he had eaten enough, lunch was over and it was time for cricket. "We'll go to the Long Gallery," he announced.

Accompanied by two footmen, Louis, with his cricket bat under his arm, followed the king..

They came to large double doors leading onto a wide patio and beyond that the green lawn he had seen on arrival. He expected the guards at the doors to open them so the king and his entourage could walk outside, but the king marched resolutely on. At last, they came to the Long Gallery – tall windows down one side and paintings of the king's forebears and their wives hanging on the opposite wall. The gallery was long enough to accommodate three huge fireplaces, all of which were burning brightly, even though it appeared sunny and warm outside.

"Now, Ludwig, this is where you are going to teach me to play."

"But, Your Majesty, it is better to play cricket outside."

"That's what you think," replied the king, "but if you

teach me here, the ball won't go far if I hit it."

It was obvious to Louis that the king would not be moved.

"Of course, Your Majesty, but we need a wicket."

"A wicket? What's a wicket? Or are you saying I'm wicked?"

"No, sir," said Louis quickly. "You're obviously not wicked. A wicket is something I try to hit with the ball when I bowl to you – that means a special kind of throw, nothing to do with what you put food or water in. If you fail to strike the ball and the ball hits the wicket, you're out and I go in to bat."

"I don't really understand what you're saying." The king, scratching his head and almost dislodging his precarious crown, thought for a moment. "Why don't we use my throne as the wicket. It's wide and deep enough to catch a stray ball."

Louis looked doubtful. He had never used a throne as a wicket. But there was always a first time.

"Come on, Ludwig, hurry up. We haven't got all day and it will be suppertime soon. I'm already getting hungry."

Louis showed the king how to hold the bat and, equally important, how to stand sideways to the flight of the ball. The king suggested he should take his breastplate off but Louis recommended he keep it on. After all, he had brought a real cricket ball, red and hard, not a tennis ball. If he struck the king on his chest and he wasn't wearing his breastplate, he might well have an injured monarch on his hands.

Taking long strides, Louis measured the length of the imaginary pitch, used his jacket, which he folded and placed on the floor, as his bowling crease and finally removed the wig the king had insisted he should wear. It had been itchy. Now he had a good excuse to take it off.

And thus the game of cricket began. Every ball Louis bowled the king missed, making absolutely no connection with the bat. More often than not, the ball landed on the soft cushion of the king's throne. His Majesty became increasingly frustrated, despite Louis's best efforts to advise patience. Once more he urged the king to keep his eye on the ball. The next delivery struck the monarch on the shin.

"Ouch, Ludwig, be careful," he said, rubbing his shin vigorously. "I need my legs."

"Sorry, Your Majesty." Louis wondered if there was a punishment for bruising a royal limb and, if so, how severe it was.

"I want a ball I can hit," shouted the king.

39

This time, Louis prepared to bowl a slower ball, aiming it as accurately as he could at the monarch's bat.

"Keep your eye on the ball as it approaches you. If you think you're going to strike it, play it down to the floor," he said as the ball left his fingers.

But the king hadn't a clue what Louis meant. Instead, he closed his eyes, spun around twice and for the first time his bat somehow connected with the ball.

Thwack! The king struck the ball with such force that it hit the marble bust of the queen's grandmother, taking the head with it. Gathering speed from the ricochet, the ball then smashed to smithereens a large  ornamental porcelain vase on a table between two of the windows. It finally ended up at the feet of the king's personal valet, who picked it up and lobbed it at his lord and master, who in turn swept it clean

through one of the windows – glass everywhere.

Suddenly, there was a commotion. The queen, just returned from riding in the forest, came running towards the

Long Gallery to find out what was going on. The entire palace staff seemed to be heading their way, from major-domo and lady-in-waiting to bootboy and scullery maid.

Though thrilled he had hit the ball twice, the king surveyed with apprehension the damage he had caused.

"Quick, Ludwig, you and I had better scarper, find somewhere to hide. If the queen finds out I have decapitated her grandmother and smashed a vase from her great-grandmother she'll be furious. I will be in serious trouble. Bodo, don't tell her where we're going. Promise?"

"Yes, sire," replied the king's personal valet.

"Yes you will or yes you won't?" barked the king.

"I won't, sire."

"Good, you'll keep your head in that case."

The king turned and ran down the corridor, then

another and yet another, followed by Louis and Lady St George, who had lifted her skirts and was enjoying the exercise and excitement after two hundred and fifty years stuck on canvas. The queen's voice was getting closer and louder.

"Ludwig, I've got to get out of the palace, back to the safety of my frame."

Louis caught sight of the carriage in which they had arrived earlier in the day.

"Look, Your Majesty, the coach. We just need to go through this door and across the patio to reach it."

"Well spotted, Ludwig!"

The three escapees – the king, Lady St George and Louis – sprinted towards the carriage and flung themselves inside.

"Get going immediately," the king ordered the coachman. "Back to where you found us this morning. Hurry, man!"

The carriage heaved forward and hurtled off down the driveway in a shower of pebbles, chased by the queen carrying the head of her decapitated grandmother and shaking her fist. They soon left her behind.

"That was a close shave! But what great fun," said Lady St George.

"Indeed it was," replied the king, still out of breath. "I enjoyed myself. Thank you, Ludwig, for teaching me how to hit a ball. I'll have another go at some stage but perhaps you're right, it's better to play outside. I must confess, though, I had great pleasure in seeing the bust beheaded." He roared with laughter.

Louis said nothing. He was too amazed by what he had seen and done. The only sadness was that he had not had his promised pain au chocolat.

❀ ❀ ❀ ❀ ❀

The alarm clock buzzed. It was seven o'clock, time to rise and soon time for breakfast. Louis got up quietly. His sister was still asleep. No strange clothes lay at the end of his bed. He put on his dressing gown and slippers and stole along the corridor. From the window, he could see no carriage and horses, only two cars, his mother's and his grandfather's. He went downstairs and entered the dining room. His usual breakfast was waiting for him, and not only that: on a side plate was a plump pain au chocolat from the village deli.

As he took his seat at the table, Louis looked up at the paintings. Lady St George smiled at him from her golden frame high above the doorway to the TV room. As for  the king, he too smiled from his own lofty square perch. Louis concentrated on eating his breakfast, just in case it might suddenly disappear. As he munched on his deliciously fresh pain au chocolat and his grandfather pottered in the kitchen, he thought he heard a voice behind him.

"Yesterday was really good fun, Ludwig. But, as Lady St George said, we had a close shave with the queen. I don't know what she would have done if she had collared me. I think I'll resume a life of peace and quiet for a while. See you around."

Louis turned and looked once more at King Ludwig. He had his usual morose expression. Yet Louis was sure he had heard his voice. Then again, as his grandfather often said, things are not always what they seem.

Chapter
5

Several days passed without disturbance to Louis's sleep and – most important of all – no further royal theft of his breakfast. As the end of his holiday approached, everything was as he expected it to be. And his mind was already preoccupied with going back to school.

On Friday evening – the last night of his stay at his grandfather's house – he was in bed by eight o'clock as usual, his things already half packed for a prompt departure by car after breakfast the next day. He was sure it would be a special breakfast. In fact, the secret had already been divulged in a snatched conversation he had overheard in the kitchen. He was therefore pretty confident that after the usual fruit and yogurt he would enjoy a pain au chocolat instead of a croissant. The latter was tasty but for him a pain au chocolat was the ultimate treat. As he rarely enjoyed this supreme delicacy at home in London – where it was replaced each day by a boring slice of toast and butter – he would savour every morsel.

It was four o'clock in the morning – at least, that was the time on his bedside clock – when he was awoken by a rustling sound. He instantly recognised the familiar silhouette of Ludwig, once more out of his picture frame, at the foot of the bed. Louis could tell it was him because in the light of the small candle the king was holding he saw the crown perched even more precariously on the top of the monarch's grey wig. But there was someone else standing beside him – taller and more substantial in girth, wearing what appeared in the flickering candlelight to be a blue cloak covered in silver fleurs-de-lys. The figure's face was half obscured by long black ringlets. Louis, being an acute observer of the world around him and possessing an excellent memory, suddenly realised that this apparition – he could think of no better description – bore a remarkable similarity to the image of King Louis XIV of France depicted on the fridge magnet in his grandfather's kitchen.

As Louis peered in disbelief, the two monarchs jostled one another.

"He's mine. I found him first," insisted King Ludwig. "He and I are friends. You can't have him. Besides, you are dead. You died four years before I was born! You don't exist any more."

"Oh yes I can have him, and I will. I may be dead but like the sunrise my spirit keeps going every day. Anyway, I was grander than you'll ever be. I had more territory than you will ever possess. And most important of all, I was le Roi Soleil, the Sun King. Apollo the Sun God was my personal emblem. So, Ludwig, monarch of a minor German kingdom, step aside. Whether I be dead or alive, I command it!"

"Ghosts don't command living monarchs. You've had your go. Push off," replied Ludwig.

The two monarchs continued to barge and shove each other.

"Stop it, both of you," said Louis. "If you carry on, you'll wake my sister. And if you do that, my mother will be cross – very cross. I'll get up and meet you  downstairs. Then you can decide which of you has precedence for whatever you want me to do. But you had better decide quickly because in three hours I am due to have my breakfast and, if it please you both, I don't want to miss it – or lose it."

The two kings were taken aback by Louis's admonishment. Neither was used to such a rebuke from a young boy. Harrumphing, both scuttled towards the bedroom door, where they became wedged trying to shoulder through first. Louis shook his head.

When he entered the dining room downstairs, the two monarchs were still bickering. Louis didn't know what to do. Suddenly, Lady St George, tired of the disturbance, stepped down from her frame.

"I wish to suggest, Your Majesties, that as you, Ludwig, have enjoyed young Louis's company twice, perhaps it's time for his Royal Sunship to show Louis his grand Palace of Versailles."

Louis XIV smiled in triumph. "Well spoken, Madame Saint George," he said, giving her name the full French treatment. "Good sensible English pragmatism. By the way, madame, I like your décolleté dress. It suits you well."

"Thank you for the compliment, sire, but should you not concentrate your attention on young Louis? It's less than three hours until his breakfast. If he's not back in time, there will be a tremendous kerfuffle and I'm afraid you'll get the blame."

Loath to suffer further reprimand, the Sun King nodded in agreement. After all, he had never in his life liked being kept waiting. Speed had been his watchword. It should be so on this occasion.

"It's not fair," grumbled King Ludwig. "Why should I give way to a ghastly ghost like you?"

"Hush, Ludwig. It is decided. Stop muttering and come with me. My invitation of course extends to you, Madame Saint George."

The Sun King drew himself up to his full height, waved his gold sceptre tipped with the emblem of the sun, and in a flash they were soaring across the dark sky in a huge winged chariot pulled by eight black horses – a chariot even greater in size and magnificence than the ones young Louis had seen illustrated in books about Ancient Rome, the horses caparisoned in the Sun King's gilded livery.

Arriving on the Palace of Versaille's southern terrace in morning sunshine, Louis was overawed by the sheer scale of what he saw – the colossal palace edifice on one side and on the other, steps leading down to a mighty fountain and further steps to another beyond that. The palace gardens with their trees, flowers and finely cut lawns continued as far as the eye could see.

"You should have brought your cricket bat, Louis," chuckled King Ludwig as they alighted from the chariot. "We could have had another game on one of the lawns down there. I might have scored some runs this time without causing any damage."

"Be quiet," whispered Lady St George. "The Sun King is about to speak."

Louis the Great, now surrounded by courtiers and ladies in fine dresses, turned to his young namesake.

"You, my boy, will be the bearer of my footstool, preceding me as I progress through the Hall of Mirrors to my throne. When I stamp my right foot, you will stop and put the stool down in front of wherever I choose to sit. I will rest my foot on it. When I stand up, you will bow, pick up the footstool and process before me until I stamp again. Do you understand that, mon petit Louis?"

"I think I do, Your Majesty. But how will I always know when you wish me to stop? I might not hear your foot tap."

The king smiled. "Simple, petit Louis. You walk

backwards, facing me."

Louis gulped at the thought of what lay ahead.

"Bouton," said the king, turning to the attendant closest to him, "quickly dress this young man. As soon as he's ready and I have got myself sumptuously attired, we will gather at the entrance to the Hall of Mirrors. Vite, man, petit Louis is in a hurry, as am I."

"And what about me?" growled King Ludwig.

"You will remain a respectful distance behind me, old fossil, bowing and scraping."

"But you're a ghost. Why should I show deference to a king who has been and gone?"

"Dear old Ludwig, it's simple. Just do as you are told! If you don't, I'll ask my great-grandson Louis XV to nab your lands. He's already on the loose in the Low Countries."

Ludwig decided he had better say no more.

"And me, sire, what should I do?" asked Lady St George.

"You, madame, will walk close behind me and when the appropriate moment comes you will sing for us. I am told you have a beautiful voice."

Young Louis thought he saw her blush.

In the blink of an eye, Louis was in place, dressed in white breeches, a red waistcoat and a blue knee-length coat embroidered with silver acorns. On his head sat a grey wig tied back in a ponytail. A servant handed him the small elaborately carved yellow footstool. The

marshal of the court blew his horn and the royal entourage disassembled and re-formed in two columns some ten metres apart, dukes, counts, marquises and gentlemen along the right side of the Hall, and ladies of the court along the left. At the head of one column were the royal musicians, and of the other, the standard bearers. In front of them was a lone courtier holding up high a staff adorned with the emblem of Apollo, the Sun God. And facing the emblem stood Louis, looking nervously down the gleaming expanse of parquet between the two columns waiting to see the great doors open and the Sun King to emerge.

Chapter
6

Once more the marshal blew his horn and then came a roll of drums. The doors opened to reveal the king, draped in a long sapphire-blue ermine-lined cape covered in jewels and the fleur-de-lys motif. He paused with dramatic panache, then began to walk slowly towards him, flanked by an armada of matelots, some beating drums, others blowing whistles, all of them dressed in black silver-buckled shoes, white stockings, loose calf-length blue bell-bottom pantaloons, short tight-fitting red jackets and black tricorns. As the king processed, the matelots behind him rocked from side to side with the stately beat of the music, now enhanced by

the flutes and oboes of the court musicians. Occasionally, they would twirl. The courtiers and ladies in each column bowed and curtsied as the monarch approached.

Louis felt his knees begin to knock, his heart thumping five times faster than the beat of the drums of the advancing matelots. All thought of the pain au chocolat had been forgotten.

The king approached the emblem of the Sun God. The bearer of the effigy, sensing the monarch close behind him, mouthed the word "Now," and on this instruction Louis, clutching the stool fiercely, began to walk backwards, nothing between him and the Sun King but the single courtier, holding the  effigy aloft. It was not easy, walking backwards in a straight line in step with the music while watching the king's right foot. And the light was dazzling – bright sun streaming through the floor-to-ceiling windows and reflected in the seventeen mirrored arches. Above were vast, richly coloured frescoes. It was hard for Louis to keep focused on what he had to do.

Suddenly, the king stopped and stamped his right foot. The music ceased and a golden chair was placed behind him. As the king sat down, Louis stepped forward and placed the stool beneath the hovering royal foot.

"Madame Saint George, please sing for us."

She appeared from amid the matelots and unhesitating, with serene composure, sang a beautiful aria from A Royal Mass for the Sun King, written by the king's master composer. Louis was transfixed, as was the king, by the crystalline tone of her soprano voice. She began slowly and then quickened in time with a beat set by Monsieur Lully, the composer himself, tapping his great baton on the floor to guide the court musicians. The notes Lady St George sang seemed to float featherlike in the air. Once more the beat slowed and yet again accelerated. All eyes were on her. At the end of the aria, she curtsied deeply.

"Merci, Madame Saint George, c'était merveilleux. Please accompany us farther. We wish to hear from you again."

She curtsied once more.

The king switched his gaze to Louis and rose from his golden chair. The young Louis ran forward and picked up the footstool, once more walking backwards as the royal procession continued, to an even louder musical rendition of the March of the Gentlemen and Ladies, towards the far end of the Hall of Mirrors. There, on a dais, stood the throne of France, above it an enormous representation of the sun. Louis, conscious that the throne must be close behind him, watched the king's feet even more intently. In a fresh burst of music dominated by trumpets, the monarch stopped. He beckoned Louis.

"Petit Louis, when I am seated and you have placed the footstool before me, your task for the day will be over. You've done well to step back in time to be with me. I hope to see you again soon. You have a great future at my court and so do you, Madame Saint George. But now, madame, please enchant us by singing once more. Then you and petit Louis may leave. I hope I have not detained him too long and that he will be back in England in time for his breakfast. When we next meet we shall have breakfast here at Versailles. We provide more than pain au chocolat." The king roared with laughter, his courtiers following his cue.

Lady St George sang, this time an episode from the story of Orpheus. When she had finished, Bouton, the attendant who had dressed Louis on his arrival, led them to a small carriage drawn by four white horses, prancing restlessly, ready for departure. On the door was the emblem of the Sun King. Once more they sped across the sky.

♔ ♔ ♔ ♔ ♔

Louis woke shortly before seven o'clock. There was no one at the end of his bed and his sister, Agnes, was still asleep. He got up quietly. With his mind still full of the sights and sounds of Versailles, he put on his dressing gown and slippers and went downstairs. His breakfast was waiting for him. He looked up at the portrait of King Ludwig IX. The usual grumpy expression had darkened into a scowl. When his grandfather went into the kitchen, Louis thought he heard muttering.

"How could you do that to me? Allow me to be humiliated by that puffed-up preening peacock Louis, who believed he was the incarnation of the sun. And you, madame, in the frame above the door, you made it even worse – singing for a ghost! How could you do that? I need some yogurt – you know, that delicious white stuff I had before – and some blueberries to calm my temper. I wanted to take your breakfast this morning but madame forbade me. Goodness me, I'm so hungry."

Hearing his grandfather's footsteps, Louis looked at Ludwig and whispered, "I have to go home soon. Perhaps next time."

"Did you say something, Louis?" his grandfather asked, emerging from the kitchen.

"It was nothing," he replied. "Just talking to myself."

Chapter
7

When he left his grandfather's house to return to London, Louis had an idea what his story would be about. Back home, a surprise awaited him. His mother announced she had just received a text message from the school to say that the second half of term would begin one day later than planned because of the unexpected need for an extra inset day. Louis smiled. His imagination had finally turned up and done him proud. He was at last ready to write a story none of his classmates would have thought of. He assured his mother, when she came to tuck him up, that all would be well.

The next morning, immediately after breakfast – no croissant or pain au chocolat, just an unexciting

slice of toast and butter – Louis went to his bedroom and opened his English exercise book. He read the words in red ink.

"I'll show you, Webby," he said out loud. "I've got a story that's never been heard before. It's all about what happened to me – no one else."

For the next hour, Louis wrote furiously, remembering every detail of what had happened to him, about the boy who carried King Louis XIV's footstool. Of course, it would seem an improbable tale to others, but be that as it may, he knew it had actually happened – at least he thought it had. He had carried

the footstool of the Sun King himself and he had done so because another king, Ludwig IX of Hesse-Darmstadt, had eaten his breakfast – an example of one thing leading to another, as his mother often said to him when things went wrong, though in this case it had been the opposite.

After checking his spelling and underlining the many new words he had used with the help of his dictionary, he closed the exercise book, a smile of pride on his face, and put it in his school bag. He had finally done it – thanks to his friend imagination.

His mother was in the kitchen.

"Have you written your story, Louis?"

"Yes, I have."

"What's it about? Can I read it?"

"I can't tell you what it's about. I will after school."

"All very mysterious, Master Louis. It had better be good. You've taken long enough over it."

Louis smiled enigmatically.

School reopened and Louis handed in his story. Two days later Mr Webb began his English class.

"Thank you for your half-term stories. I've read them all. There was an interesting selection. But there was one that was very good – excellent, even – and worthy of the high mark I've given it." He paused. Tension rose in the classroom as Mr Webb surveyed the expectant faces before him.

"Louis, you have written an extraordinary story. Such originality. I'd like you to read it to the class. Please come to the front."

Sitting beside Mr Webb,

Louis proudly began his story of the king who ate my breakfast.

Later that evening, still basking in the praise his mother had lavished on him over supper, he was surfing his iPad before bath time. Suddenly, the emblem of the Sun God filled the screen. It winked and Louis was sure he heard it whisper, "À bientot." As the image slowly began to fade, in the corner of the screen appeared King Ludwig, waving his arms, his crown still askew, uttering the words, "Auf Wiedersehen, Ludwig."

Louis waved to both his royal friends. He would not forget them.

He decided that when he next returned to his grandfather's house for a holiday he would tell King Ludwig and Lady St George all about his high mark and perhaps, in gratitude, somehow secretly leave out two bowls of yogurt and blueberries, one for each of them. After all, it was always best to keep on the right side of royalty and ladies with beautiful voices.

The End

Author's Note

Three notable people inspired this story.

The first is Ludwig IX of Hesse-Darmstadt, who ruled from 1768 to 1790. His portrait, painted in the latter part of his reign, hangs on our dining-room wall in Norfolk. Though he was not a particularly distinguished head of state, he has a benevolent smile on his face (unlike his counterpart in the story), seeming to approve of what's going on below. He has over the years become a close friend of the family.

Adjacent to him on the wall is a painting of Frederick the Great of Prussia, a contemporary of Ludwig, completed in his younger years. With his fine tricorn hat and richly embroidered jacket, he is the embodiment of Prussian self-confidence and superiority, which he put to good use pinching the territories of other monarchs. Even late at night I've never overheard Ludwig and Frederick engaged in conversation – the latter perhaps too standoffish and the former anxious not to offend his neighbour for fear of losing his land. Frederick has not appeared in this story, beyond a disparaging reference from Ludwig, but I have a feeling he may intervene on another occasion.

The second source of inspiration is Louis XIV of France, who portrayed himself as the Sun King. Featuring on a fridge magnet in our kitchen, he is imposing in posture, looking at the viewer with an uncompromising eye – very much in the mode of Apollo, the Greek God of the Sun. We bought the magnet last year on a return visit to Versailles, where we spent hours on a warm, cloudless September day strolling the length and breadth of the palace gardens while listening to the music of Jean-Baptiste Lully and Marc-Antoine Charpentier, composers to le Roi Soleil, coming from artfully concealed speakers amongst the trees. It was easy to imagine ourselves onlookers as elegant, elaborately coiffed ladies in décolleté dresses and men in stylish frock coats promenaded in the company of the great Louis.

The third inspiration – the most important of all – is my grandson Louis. When he comes to stay in the school holidays with his siblings, his greatest pleasure seems to be the breakfast I serve: yogurt and an array of fresh fruit followed usually by a croissant or toasted teacake but occasionally by a pain au chocolat.

So, like a chef, I took three different ingredients called Louis and blended them into the story you have just read. I hope it was tasty.

Edward Glover

North Norfolk

Tuesday 7 April 2020

Acknowledgements

I wish to thank warmly five people who helped me with this book.

First, Sue Tyley, my copy-editor, who once more applied her professional skills to ensure the ingredients of my concoction were at their best.

Second, Tracy Hagan, my equally skilful illustrator, who put to work her superb presentational expertise to help tell the story.

Third, my wife, Audrey, who listened patiently as the story unfolded and made some useful suggestions.

Fourth, Justin Davis, from my publisher Blue Falcon Publishing, who brought the story to your hands.

And finally, young Louis himself, because if he did not enjoy my breakfasts there would have been no story.

About the Author

Edward Glover was born in London. After gaining a history degree followed by an MPhil at Birkbeck, University of London, he embarked on a career in the British diplomatic service, during which his overseas postings included Washington DC, Berlin, Brussels and the Caribbean. He subsequently advised on foreign ministry reform in post-invasion Iraq, Kosovo and Sierra Leone. For seven years he headed a one-million-acre rainforest-conservation project in South America, on behalf of the Commonwealth Secretariat and the Government of Guyana.

With an interest in 16th- and 18th-century history, baroque music and 18th-century art, in 2012 Edward was encouraged by the purchase of two paintings and a passport to try his hand at writing historical fiction.

Edward and his wife, former Foreign & Commonwealth Office lawyer and leading international human rights adviser Dame Audrey Glover, now live in Norfolk, a place that gives him further inspiration for his writing.

He is chair of the Foreign, Commonwealth and Development Office Association; was until recently a trustee of the Welsh environmental charity Size of

Wales; sits on the board of the King's Lynn Preservation Trust; and is an associate fellow of the University of Warwick Yesu Persaud Centre for Caribbean Studies.

When he isn't writing, Edward is an avid tennis player and completed the 2014 London Marathon, raising £7,000 for Ambitious about Autism.

Other Books by Edward Glover
(Note:- these are not childrens books)

THE HERZBERG TRILOGY

Book 1: The Music Book

A young English woman, on the run from her father, and a retired Prussian military officer sent to England by King Frederick the Great are plunged into the London demi-monde and a pursuit across Europe in search of fulfilment. The young woman's music book bears witness to what unfolds.

Book 2: Fortune's Sonata

English by birth, Prussian by marriage, rebellious by nature, the beautiful Arabella von Deppe steers her family through turbulent historical times in this thrilling story of love and loss, betrayal and revenge, ambition and beliefs, friendship and fate. With music as her inspiration and a murderer as her friend, she proves a worthy adversary of Fortune as she weathers winds beyond her control.

Book 3: A Motif of Seasons

Two powerful 19th-century English and Prussian families are still riven by the consequences of an ancestral marriage – one that bequeathed venomous division, rivalry and hatred. Three beautiful women – each ambitious and musically gifted – seek to break these inherited shackles of betrayal, revenge and cruelty in their pursuit of sexual freedom and love. But the past proves a formidable and vicious opponent.

The Executioner's House

Germany, October 1946. The Nuremburg war crimes tribunal has just ended. Major Richard Fortescue, previously part of the British prosecution team, is returning to London when he encounters Karin Eilers, a young German woman with a dark past. Against the backdrop of war-devastated Berlin and the continuing search for former Nazis, their brief affair and a mysterious black notebook make them unwitting pawns in a deadly game of intrigue and betrayal played by British and Soviet intelligence. What wartime secrets will the notebook unravel? Who else will become a victim of the battle for its possession?

The Lute Player

Mystery, obsession, rage, joy, demons, death, secrets and a lute. All to be found on Johannes' journey – a father's search, an artist's mission, a lost soul's quest – where nothing, especially Khadra the lute player, is ever quite what it seems. Venture beyond the borders of the Herzberg trilogy and The Executioner's House to an intensely personal landscape in which fantasy, fable and metaphysics overlay ancient civilisations, and threads of history, music and art weave through a vividly conjured seeker's story.

Dark Obsession

On a golden sunlit evening in the summer of 1875, the glimpse of a young woman on the river marks the beginning of the obsession of a man of wealth and influence, its darkening shadow spreading from southern France to Paris, to Cochinchina and Spain, altering lives. For some it will be fatal; some will find freedom. A former detective, a society beauty, an imperial concubine, a painter, as well as the girl herself, are each subject to its thrall – and all have passions of their own. Victim or agent. Guilty or innocent. You decide.